For Mom and Dad—BS

W

PENGUIN WORKSHOP
An Imprint of Penguin Random House LLC, New York

Copyright © 2020 by Benson Shum. All rights reserved. Published by Penguin Workshop, an imprint of Penguin Random House LLC, New York. PENGUIN and PENGUIN WORKSHOP are trademarks of Penguin Books Ltd, and the W colophon is a registered trademark of Penguin Random House LLC. Manufactured in China.

Visit us online at www.penguinrandomhouse.com.

Library of Congress Cataloging-in-Publication Data is available upon request.

ISBN 9780593222935 (pbk)   10 9 8 7 6 5 4 3 2 1
ISBN 9780593222942 (hc)   10 9 8 7 6 5 4 3 2 1

Alex's
Good Fortune

by Benson Shum

Penguin Workshop

When Alex wakes up and remembers what day it is, she puts on her red shirt and red headband.

"Happy Chinese New Year!" she says.

"Can I invite Ethan over for the holiday?"

"Of course," Mom replies.

Once Ethan arrives, they join the Chinese New Year parade.

Ethan helps lift the dragon.

Alex carries the staff to lead the way.

Together they make the dragon dance.

In the streets, the sounds of drums, cymbals, and firecrackers fill the air.

Dum da Dum

Dum Dum!

Ethan waves the dragon up and down.
Alex holds the staff.

"What does it all mean?" asks Ethan.
"The dragon dance brings good luck
to everyone," says Alex.

After the parade, friends and family gather at Alex's house.
Everyone exchanges wishes for a healthy and happy year.

Auntie Lin hands Alex and Ethan red envelopes for luck.
"Gōng xǐ fā cái," says Auntie Lin.
"Xīn xiǎng shì chéng," says Alex.

There is money inside!

Uncle Tai paints red banners for the front door.
Alex and Ethan help paint.

Stroke and sweep,

stroke and sweep.

They hang them up to wish everyone peace all year round.

Chinese New Year also brings Alex's least
favorite tradition.

Before the start of the new year, Alex had
to clean her room, to wash away bad luck.
After that, she swept the floor.

Ethan had offered to help, and wiped the table for his friend.

Nai Nai makes dumplings in the kitchen.
Alex and Ethan help wrap them.

Fold and pinch,
fold and pinch.

Alex likes them fried.

Ethan likes them steamed.

Chinese New Year dishes have many meanings.

Fish for prosperity.

Noodles for long life.

Dumplings for wealth.

Chicken for family.

And lots and lots of candies for good fortune!

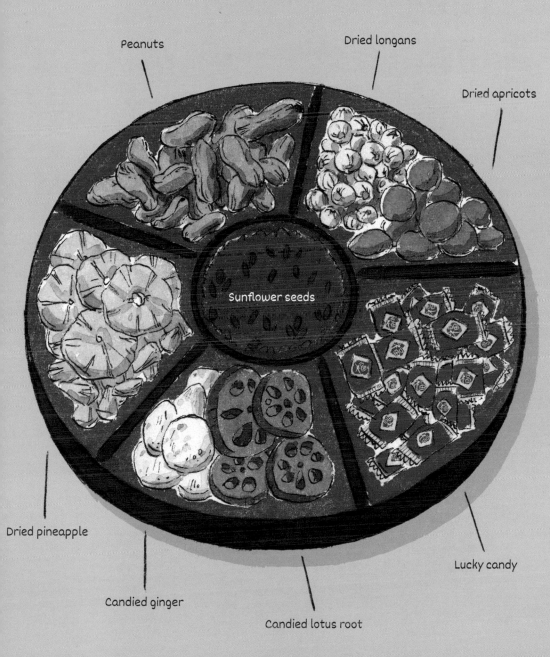

Peanuts

Dried longans

Dried apricots

Sunflower seeds

Dried pineapple

Candied ginger

Candied lotus root

Lucky candy

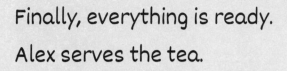

Finally, everything is ready.
Alex serves the tea.

Ethan carries in the rice.

It's time for the most delicious tradition . . .

23

. . . the grand banquet!

Everyone gathers to share dumplings, noodles, and many other dishes.

Alex's favorite tradition is the lantern
festival, which falls on the fifteenth day
of the celebration.
To mark the end of Chinese New Year,
friends and families go to the park to enjoy it.

Alex and Ethan grab their lanterns
and hang them on the tallest tree.
The lanterns shine like stars in the sky.

"Thank you for sharing the holiday
with me, Alex," Ethan says.

"I'm glad we got to celebrate together,"
Alex replies.

"Happy Chinese New Year!" they shout.

"Xīn nián kuài lè!"

Chinese New Year is a time for family and friends to celebrate with music, dancing, cooking, and lots of eating. Food is a big part of the Chinese New Year festivities. There are many dishes to prepare and lots of goodies to eat during the celebration.

The color red is seen throughout the New Year, from banners and lucky envelopes to clothing and headbands. Red symbolizes good luck.

There is also the story of the Chinese zodiac. The zodiac calendar is a twelve-year cycle, and each year is represented by an animal. Legend says that long ago the Jade Emperor, on his birthday, decided to select twelve animals to guard the heavenly gates. There was to be a great race across a fast-flowing river. The first twelve animals to cross would win.

Rat arrived first, then Ox, Tiger, Rabbit, Dragon, Snake, Horse, Sheep, Monkey, Rooster, Dog, and finally Pig. These twelve became the animals on the Chinese zodiac calendar.

Each animal has its own unique personality. It is believed that if you are born in the Year of the Rat, for example, you will have the Rat's character traits.

Rat

Quick-witted
Intelligent
Natural-born leaders

Ox

Strong
Stubborn
Hardworking

Tiger

Brave
Reckless
Intense

Rabbit

Polite
Affectionate
Sincere

Dragon

Fearless
Creative
Ambitious

Snake

Intuitive
Wise
Calm

Horse

Independent
Impatient
Positive

Sheep

Gentle
Patient
Easygoing

Monkey

Adventurous
Active
Curious

Rooster

Trustworthy
Talented
Practical

Dog

Loyal
Diligent
Generous

Pig

Problem solvers
Humble
Honest

Chinese New Year Wishes

Gōng xǐ fā cái

(say: gong zee fah tsai)

Wishing you wealth and prosperity.

Xīn xiǎng shì chéng

(say: sin see-ang shee che-eng)

May all your wishes come true.

Shēn tǐ jiàn kāng

(say: shen tee jian kang)

Wishing you good health.

Nián nián yǒu yú

(say: nian nian yo yu)

May you have abundance every year.

Xīn nián kuài lè

(say: sheen nian kwai luh)

Happy New Year.